HANS DE BEER was born in 1957 in Muiden, a small town near Amsterdam, in Holland.
He began to draw when he went to school, mostly when the lessons got too boring.
In college he studied history, but he was drawing so many pictures during the lectures
that he decided to become an artist. He went on to study illustration
at the Rietveld Academy of Art in Amsterdam.
Hans de Beer's first book, *Little Polar Bear*, was very popular around the world.
The book has been published in 18 languages. Hans had so much fun
illustrating picture books that he did more of them.
He likes to draw polar bears, cats, walruses, elephants, and moles.
His books have received many prizes, among them the first prize from
an international jury of children in Bologna, Italy.

Copyright © 1987, 1999 by NordSüd Verlag AG, CH-8005 Zürich, Switzerland.
First published in Switzerland under the title *Kleiner Eisbär – Wohin fährst du, Lars?*
English text copyright © 1987, 1999 by Hans de Beer.

First published in the United States, Great Britain, Canada, Australia, and New Zealand in 1987
by NorthSouth Books Inc., an imprint of NordSüd Verlag AG, CH-8005 Zürich, Switzerland.
This edition first published in 2016.

Distributed in the United States by NorthSouth Books Inc., New York 10016.

Library of Congress Cataloging-in-Publication Data is available.
A CIP catalogue record for this book is available from The British Library.

ISBN: 978-0-7358-4264-9 (trade edition)
1 3 5 7 9 HC 10 8 6 4 2
ISBN: 978-0-7358-4052-2 (paperback edition)
5 7 9 PB 10 8 6

Printed in Poland by Drukarnia Interak Sp. z o.o., Czarnków, July 2016.

www.northsouth.com

Hans de Beer

LITTLE POLAR BEAR

Where are You Going Lars?

North
South

It was a big day for Lars. He was going with his father on his first hunting trip. Lars was white all over, just like his father. In fact, at the North Pole where Lars lived everything was white because it was covered in ice and snow.

Lars's father showed him how to do all kinds of things: follow tracks, swim, and dive. He talked and talked and Lars listened silently, paying close attention. Once his father disappeared underwater and stayed so long Lars began to worry. But when his father finally reappeared, he had a big fish for supper.

When it was time to go to sleep Lars's father said, "Make a big pile of snow to protect yourself from the wind, like I do."

Lars was proud of his pile, but also very tired. He quickly fell asleep, just like his father.

But during the night the ice began to crack. The piece where Lars was lying broke off.

When Lars woke up it was morning. He was all alone in the middle of the sea. It was getting warmer and warmer and the piece of ice and Lars's pile of snow were getting smaller and smaller.

When the ice was almost completely melted Lars saw a big barrel drifting by. Luckily Lars was able to reach the barrel and climb on top of it.

Then a storm began to rage. As Lars clung to his bobbing barrel he missed his father and his pile of snow more and more.

After the storm Lars drifted on the sea for a long time. At last he saw land but could not see any snow or ice. Almost everything was green and the sun was very warm. Lars carefully slid off the barrel and stepped onto the beach.

The beach was hot and yellow. It burned Lars's paws. He ran to a river nearby. But just as he was about to plunge in, a very big, tan animal sprung out of the water.

"Booo!" it said.

Lars quickly ran to hide.

"I was only joking," called the big, tan animal. "I'm Henry, the hippopotamus. Who are you and why are you so white?"

Lars didn't know the answer to the last question. "Where I come from, everything is white," he said.

He told Henry about his long journey and asked him how he could get back to his father.

Henry listened sympathetically, but he seemed confused. He wiggled his ears and squirmed and finally said, "The only one who can help you is Marcus, the eagle. He has travelled all over the world. He will know where you come from and how you can get back there. But we'll have to cross the river, go through the jungle, and climb the mountains to reach him."

Lars was happy to go, but when he looked at the river he said, "The only problem is that I can't swim very well yet."

"No problem at all," said Henry and laughed. "Climb on my back. I won't sink."

Lars was astonished by all the things he saw in the jungle. Henry patiently explained everything. Lars especially liked the tall, brown stalks that Henry called trees. They were such fun to climb!

In one brown stalk sat a funny green animal, which suddenly turned white, just like Lars.

"It's a chameleon," Henry said. "It can change its color."

Lars thought that was a handy thing to be able to do.

At the edge of the jungle, the mountains began. It was a bit cooler and Lars felt more comfortable. Henry found climbing difficult, but Lars helped by telling him where to step.

After a while Henry was exhausted.

"That's enough for today," he said. "Tomorrow we will continue. Let's rest here and look at the nice view."

As Lars looked out over the land and sea, he began to feel homesick.

"Cheer up," said Henry. "You'll be home again soon."

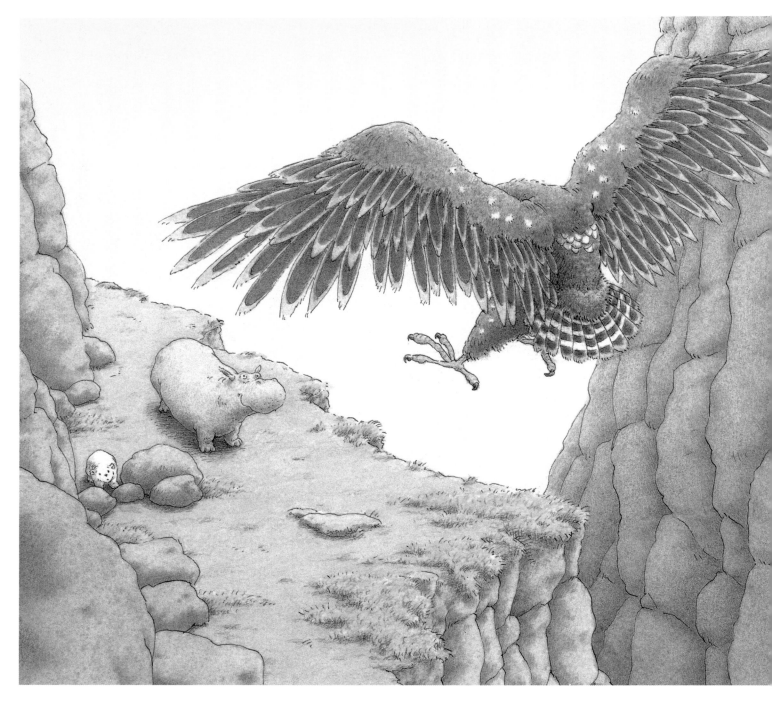

The next day they climbed higher. Henry had to stop often to catch his breath. But at last he called, "Here comes Marcus!" as a huge bird swooped down near Lars. Lars ducked.

"Don't be afraid," said Henry. "Marcus seems gruff, but he's really quite friendly."

Henry said good morning to Marcus and politely explained why they had come. The eagle looked at Lars and then said, "Well, well, a polar bear in the tropics! You're a long way from home aren't you, young man? Fortunately I can arrange your passage back. Tomorrow morning I will have Samson fetch you from the beach."

"Thank you very much, sir," said Lars shyly.

The next morning Henry and Lars met Marcus on the beach.

"Right on time," said Marcus proudly as a huge gray whale arrived.

Although Henry was happy for Lars, he was also sorry to see him go. "Take care of yourself," he said sadly.

"Thanks for everything, Henry," Lars called as the whale swam away.

Henry stood alone on the beach. He kept watching for a long time after Lars and the whale had disappeared.

Samson swam a long way until they were surrounded by ice and snow.

"We must be near your home now," he said.

At the same moment Lars called, "There he is, my father! Father! I'm back!"

Lars's father couldn't believe his eyes. There was Lars riding on top of a whale.

Lars's father was very tired from looking for Lars. But he wasn't too tired to catch a big fish for Samson to thank him. Samson waved as he swam away.

"And now," said Lars's father, "we must go straight home because your mother is very worried."

On the way home Lars rode on his father's back. Everything was white and he was surrounded by snow and ice. But this time Lars talked and talked while his father was silent. He told his father about all the amazing things he had seen: Henry, the tall, brown stalks, Marcus, and much more.

"You didn't meet anyone who was white?" asked his father in surprise.

"Nobody, except a chameleon," said Lars, "but that doesn't count."

Lars had to laugh by himself because his father didn't understand his joke.